THIS NOTEBOOK BELONGS TO

Made in the USA
Monee, IL
15 January 2022

88936689R00057